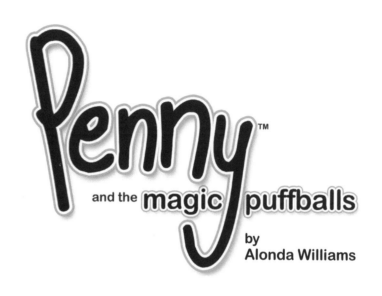

Penny™

and the **magic puffballs**

by
Alonda Williams

Published 2013 by: Glori Publishing Redmond, WA 98052
www.Gloripublishing.com

Publishing Contact: 908-578-9595
Printed in the United States of America

Library of Congress Control Number: 2013955472

ISBN 978-0-9912129-0-3

Penny and the magic puffballs
Summary : Details the adventures of Penny, a precocious little girl who discovers the magical powers of her new puffball hairstyle.

Address all inquiries to :
Alonda Williams
Email: alonda@outlook.com
For book orders visit: www.pennyandthemagicpuffballs.com

Cover and Interior Design by Kirk R. Myhre www.myhrecreative.com

message to parents

What you have in your hands is a labor of love. Penny was born out of my love for my daughter, Paris, and my desire for her to feel comfortable, confident and secure in her skin. Paris questioned why her hair was different from all of the other girls' and wondered why she couldn't wear her hair like theirs. I wanted her to understand that her hair was different but that different didn't mean bad. Little girls often notice their hair as one of the first areas of difference, and seeing this as bad can lead to a poor self-image. One night, I made up a bedtime story about a little girl named Penny who had magic puffballs in her hair. Both my daughter and my son loved it so much that they wanted to hear about Penny every night. To keep it interesting, each night I added a different adventure, and from time to time I introduced additional characters. The kids loved these stories so much that Penny became a staple in our bedtime routine. I ended up with more than 30 stories, and we enjoyed Penny's adventures for many, many years. The idea for a book came to me as I saw little girls throughout my travels with their hair styled in puffballs. I thought it would be great to be able to tell these girls the story of Penny, a little girl like them. It is my hope that through this book, other girls will see a bit of themselves in Penny and enjoy her magic puffballs.

 from Alonda

 from Tyrus

Dedicated to Paris and Tyler—my inspiration
Byron - my love
Shanna, Ahlia and Ivy – my right hand girls
Lois, Sonya, Robin, Nina, Beryl and Nikki – my supporters
Sean, Lucy, Maggie, Livi and Quinn – my local test team
Karimah for always encouraging me to go for my dreams

And to all of the little girls with Puffballs around the world
-You rock!

To my wonderfully patient wife Christy and my children who let me toil early in the mornings, working on this and other artistic endeavors, I am forever grateful.

Lexy, Nia, Troy, Tory and Donovan you guys are the color of my life.

One day, Penny, Grace and Symonne were riding on the bus home from school. Grace said, "My mom just gave me three new headbands, and she said I can give you each one because you are my best friends. I'll bring them in tomorrow, and we can all wear them."

"OK," said Symonne. "Let's all wear our hair down, and we'll wear your new headbands."

"Can you take out your braids, Penny, and just wear your hair down?" asked Grace.

"I think so," hoped Penny. "I'll ask my mom."

When Penny got home, she hugged her mother and said, "Mom, can I wear my hair down?"

"What do you mean by down?" asked her mom.

Penny exclaimed, "Mom, all the girls in my class wear their hair down."

"I want to wear my hair out—you know with no braids or anything, just out. My hair is so different and I want to be like everyone else."

Penny's mom was sad to hear that Penny wanted to change her braids. Until now, Penny had loved her braids. Penny's mom sighed deeply and looked into her daughter's eyes with love. "Oh, honey, your hair is very beautiful. Yes, it's different from your friends' hair, but different doesn't mean bad. Different is special."

"Special? What's so special about my hair?" Penny asked. "I always have it braided in the same style."

"Well, Penny, your hair can be styled in so many ways. Look at these pictures from when I was a little girl. I wore my hair in many different ways. I wore curls, braids and ponytails too. But my most favorite style of all was my puffballs. My magic puffballs. You know what, Penny? Tomorrow we are going to style your hair in puffballs."

"Really? What are puffballs, and why are they magic?" said Penny.

"You'll see," said her mom. "You'll see."

That night, Penny couldn't stop thinking about those magic puffballs. What could they be, and why did her mom say they were magic?

The next morning after Penny got dressed and ready for school, she was ready for her new hairstyle. She settled in, between her mom's knees, and her mom began taking out the braids. "Just a few more minutes and we'll be done," her mom said. Penny was so excited. She couldn't wait to see what the magic puffballs looked like.

"OK, go look in the mirror," announced Mom. Finally, thought Penny. She jumped up and ran to the mirror. The braids were gone. Instead, her hair was parted down the middle. Each side was pulled into high ponytails with her hair puffed out into soft, cotton-candy puffs.

"Oh, mom, this is so cute! I love it!" said Penny.

"These are your magic puffballs," said her mom.

"But Mom, why do you call them 'magic'? I mean, can I do magic tricks now, like pull a rabbit out of a hat?"

Mom laughed. "Well, Penny, my mom always told me that magical things could happen when I wore my puffballs. I always believed that they gave me the power to do anything. And yours will too! So don't be surprised if magical things happen when you wear your puffballs."

Penny felt excited. She couldn't wait to go to school. She skipped outside to the bus stop and waved good-bye to her mother. The magic puffballs put an extra bounce in her step. She wondered what magical things would happen today.

Penny hopped on the school bus and sat near her friends Grace and Symonne. Grace's blond hair fell to her shoulders, and she was wearing her new pink headband.

"Ooh, I like your hair," Grace blurted. "It looks like cotton candy. But brown not pink." "Yes, and it feels like cotton candy too," smiled Penny. "Can I touch them?" asked Grace. "Sure, but be careful. These are my magic puffballs," replied Penny. "Wow, magic! Cool!" said Grace. "Yes, they have magic powers, and my mom says magic things can happen when I wear my puffballs." "I can't wait to see what happens!" said Grace. Me too, thought Penny.

Penny went into Mrs. Bethea's class and hung up her backpack. As she was putting her book into her desk, she felt something stuck in the corner. She pulled out her purple pencil—the pencil that had been lost for three weeks! She loved that pencil. The magic puffballs are already working!

At lunch, Penny sat down next to Grace. "So did any magic happen yet?" said Grace.

"Well, I think so," said Penny. "You see this pencil? I lost it a long time ago and I was so sad. I mean, this is my most favorite pencil ever! I looked everywhere—in my desk, on the floor, in my backpack, EVERYWHERE. And then today, thanks to my magic puffballs, I found it. BAMMO! Just like that!"

"Wow," Grace said. "Do you really think it was the magic puffballs?"

"Absolutely!" said Penny. "That pencil was really lost, nowhere to be found."

After lunch, back in the classroom, Mrs. Bethea announced that it was time for the spelling test.

Penny was nervous. She had studied, but these words were very hard. When she practiced at home, she kept getting the same words wrong. "Oh, no," she asked herself, "is it T H E I R...or T H I E R?"

She was feeling very nervous.

When Mrs. Bethea began to read the words for the spelling test, the letters just popped into Penny's head. She didn't have to think too hard. Even the tricky words just came to her—like magic! Penny felt so great and so smart. She finished the test knowing she had done well.

When it was time to pass her paper to her neighbor Ivy, for correcting, Penny felt proud. As the teacher read the correct spelling of each word, Penny knew she had them all right. Her classmate Ivy said, "Penny, you got a 100%."

Penny was thrilled to see that she had gotten them all correct, even the tricky words. 100%! She thought, this must be the magic of my puffballs.

At recess, the girls liked to play jump rope and the boys played soccer.

"Over here, Penny, play with us," called Penny's friend Symonne.
"OK," sighed Penny.

Everyone knew Penny wasn't very good at jumping rope. In fact, she was the worst jumper and usually got the lowest score.

Grace went first. As she jumped, everyone counted. The goal was to see who could jump the longest without stumbling or tripping on the rope. "1, 2, 3, 4, 5, 6, 7...". Everyone chanted as Grace jumped. "...26, 27, 28, 29, 30..." Grace kept jumping all the way to 47. Next it was Symonne's turn. Symonne was very good at jumping and always jumped over 50 jumps. She was usually the winner. The girls counted, and Symonne kept jumping, "...33, 34, 35, 36... ," and jumping, "...51, 52, 53, 54..." Symonne jumped all the way to 65.

"OK, Penny, it's your turn."

"Aw, you know I'm not as good as you are," Penny said.

"Just give it a try," said Symonne.

"Come on, all you need is a little more practice," said Grace.

Penny rarely made it past 25 jumps. She stared at the turning ropes and thought, If there is any magic at all in these puffballs, I sure need it now.

Penny slowly approached the rope and jumped in. "1, 2, 3, 4..."

Penny started feeling good. "...21, 22, 23, 24..." Penny jumped and jumped.

"...56, 57, 58, 59..." Grace and Symonne were smiling, and their grins grew bigger with each jump."...99, 100, 101, 102..."

The girls counted higher and higher as Penny kept jumping. Soon a small crowd surrounded Penny.

"...150, 151, 152..." How high could she go? "...200, 201, 202..."

The playground was quiet except for the jump jump jump of Penny's feet.

"It's time to break it up, girls," called a teacher. "Recess is over." Penny didn't want to stop jumping. But finally Grace and Symonne stopped turning the jump rope. Everyone started clapping and clapping. "Hey, have you been practicing?" Symonne asked.

"I—uh—just got better," whispered Penny. But she knew there was only one explanation: her magic and wonderful puffballs.

On the bus ride home from school, Grace said, "Wow, those puffballs sure are magic."

"Yes, they are!" said Penny. "I wish I could have puffballs," said Grace. "Would you ask your mom if she can do my hair in puffballs?"

"I'll ask, but I'm not sure if it is possible. Puffballs are a really special thing that my hair can do. Your hair is different—not bad, just different".

When Penny got off the bus, she raced to the front door. "Mommy, Mommy, you were so right! My hair is special, and my puffballs are magic! I love them so much! I want to wear my hair like this every day!" Penny's mom smiled with satisfaction.

"Mom, you won't believe what happened today," said Penny as she walked toward her house. Her mom was not sure she was ready for what was to come. Penny began to explain everything.

Later, when Penny went to bed, she was too excited to sleep. Her mind raced ahead: What would happen tomorrow? And the next day?

Wonderful adventures were in store for Penny and her ~~puffballs.~~ magic puffballs!

power